The
Path of the Quiet Elk

A NATIVE AMERICAN ALPHABET BOOK

VIRGINIA · A · STROUD

DIAL BOOKS FOR YOUNG READERS **NEW YORK**

To my companions on the path,

and to those I have yet to meet.

Published by Dial Books for Young Readers
A Division of Penguin Books USA Inc.
375 Hudson Street • New York, New York 10014
Copyright © 1996 by Virginia A. Stroud
All rights reserved • Designed by Heather Wood
Printed in Hong Kong
First Edition
1 3 5 7 9 10 8 6 4 2

Library of Congress Cataloging in Publication Data
Stroud, Virginia A.
The path of the quiet elk : a Native American alphabet book
Virginia A. Stroud.—1st ed.
p.   cm.
ISBN 0-8037-1717-2 (trade).—ISBN 0-8037-1718-0 (library)
1. Indians of North America—Religion—Juvenile literature. 2. Indian
philosophy—North America—Juvenile literature. [1. Indians of North
America—Religion. 2. Indian philosophy—North America. 3. Alphabet.] I. Title.
E98.R3S85 1996 299′.7[E]—dc20 95-1825 CIP AC

The artwork was prepared with acrylic paint on Museum Rag paper.
It was then color-separated and reproduced in full color.

The Path of the Quiet Elk is one name for a way of looking at life where we recognize we are connected to the earth and everything on it. I learned the way of the Path of the Quiet Elk on my own walks with a medicine woman, which took place over a six-year time period.

In my story Looks Within and Wisdom Keeper, the spiritual elder of her tribe, wear everyday clothing that might have belonged to any of several Plains Indian peoples in the late 1800's, including the Cheyenne, the Arapaho, the Comanche, and the Kiowa. However, the philosophy of the story is shared by all Native American peoples, and its truths are available to all who want to learn from them.

V · A · S

Looks Within sat by the stream in the warm afternoon sunshine. She had finished her chores for the day and was busy making animal shapes from the damp clay.

Wisdom Keeper walked quietly past the stream. "Wisdom Keeper, where are you going?" called Looks Within, rinsing the clay from her hands.

"I'm taking a walk on the Path of the Quiet Elk," replied Wisdom Keeper.

"Where's the Path of the Quiet Elk?" Looks Within asked as she shook her hands dry.

Wisdom Keeper paused and gazed far into the distance. "It is not a place, but a way of learning to look at life. The elk will show us the way. Would you like to join me?"

"Yes," said Looks Within, crossing the stream.

"Before we start, you will need assistance." Wisdom Keeper raised her walking stick above her head, turned to face north, and began to sing an old song.

A Animal Helper

Then Wisdom Keeper said, "Animal Helper, please come and guide Looks Within on the Path of the Quiet Elk." The figure of a grand elk appeared in the tree line. "Follow the elk. He will assist us on the path," Wisdom Keeper said. And she and Looks Within walked side by side, following the elk's lead.

B Butterflies

Butterflies were everywhere. "Humans are like butterflies," Wisdom Keeper remarked. "The butterfly is always changing. You will change and take flight when you learn the secrets of the Path of the Quiet Elk."

C Carrying Case

She pulled a bag made of deerskin from her pouch. "You will need this." Looks Within took the soft bag in her hands.

"This is a carrying case," said Wisdom Keeper. "Use it to hold the gifts of the earth that you collect on your walk."

D Dragonflies

The two came to a small pond, where they sat for a bit. "What do you see among the cattails, Looks Within?" asked Wisdom Keeper.

"Dragonflies," said Looks Within.

Wisdom Keeper nodded. "Dragonfly's wings shine in the sun's light. She is here to remind us of the light that comes from the great Creator."

E | Eagle

Wisdom Keeper looked up in the clouds and smiled. She pointed to a black speck in the sky. "What is that, Looks Within?"

"An eagle?" answered Looks Within, peering up in the sky as the speck circled closer.

"Yes," said Wisdom Keeper. "Eagle brother is coming to carry your prayers to the Creator. He is the messenger."

F Feather

Wisdom Keeper pulled an eagle's tail feather from her bag. "This feather is for you, Looks Within," she said. "Speak to it to carry your messages up to the Creator." Looks Within put the feather into her carrying case.

G Grass

"Take your leggings off and walk in the grass. Feel the earth under your feet!" said Wisdom Keeper. "There will be days when your mind will spin with too many thoughts. By walking on the grass, you connect yourself to the earth and clear your head."

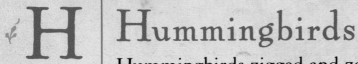 Hummingbirds

Hummingbirds zigged and zagged over the pond. "Hummingbird is a joyful little sister," Wisdom Keeper said. "She sips the sweet nectar from the flowers. Her reminder is to notice the sweetness of life and to spread it around to others." Looks Within smiled.

I | Incense

Next Wisdom Keeper walked to a cedar tree and asked the tree for permission to use its branches. Then she began to snap the tips of the boughs.

"When these branches dry, Looks Within, we will burn them. Their smoke will be an incense to help us finish our prayers."

J Jewelry

Wisdom Keeper spotted a deer antler lying on the ground. "Oh, what a treasure!" she sighed, picking it up. "Save this antler, and we will make jewelry for you later. It is a gift from the deer."

Looks Within tucked the antler in her carrying case, already planning the necklace she would make from it.

K Kernel

Wisdom Keeper stooped down and picked up a kernel of corn. She placed it in Looks Within's hand. "This kernel of corn is to remind you of the innocence of children," said Wisdom Keeper. "When children plant the seed, there is a good crop. Children's energy is not clouded with judgment. Place the kernel of corn in your carrying case, Looks Within."

L Lizard

As they walked around the pond, a lizard scurried by. Startled, Looks Within jumped back. "Don't be afraid!" said Wisdom Keeper. "Lizard is another animal helper, protecting your spirit on the path. His tail drags on the ground, erasing your footsteps so no harm can come to you. That is why the animal spirit bag you wear on your belt, the one that holds your umbilical cord, is made in the shape of a lizard."

M Medicine Wheel

As Wisdom Keeper and Looks Within continued walking, they came upon a clearing. In it sat twenty-one rocks placed in a circle. "This is someone's medicine wheel, Looks Within—a sacred space used to connect with the Great Spirit when you need an answer to a question," said Wisdom Keeper.

She pointed to the medicine wheel's doorway. "You would enter from the south, walk three times around the circle, and then sit in the center and watch for direction. You might see a sudden flash of light on the horizon, or an animal helper might appear from any of the four directions to give you guidance."

N Nature

Wisdom Keeper took from her pouch a smaller bag attached to a leather thong and decorated with porcupine quills. She hung it around Looks Within's neck. "All of nature brings us back to ourselves," she said. "In this quilled bag, put the things from nature that mirror your spirit—like this elk's tooth." She untied the tooth from her necklace and placed it in Looks Within's hand. "The elk travels far by pacing himself and using his energy to the fullest. His tooth will remind you not to fall short of your goals, Looks Within."

O  Otter

A dull *cur-plop!* sound came from the bank of the pond.

"An otter," whispered Looks Within.

"Yes. Tell me about the otter," said Wisdom Keeper.

Looks Within thought for a moment. "She's graceful, playful...and she loves both the land and water."

"Yes, what else?" asked Wisdom Keeper.

"She's trusting, happy, and silly," Looks Within finished.

"Very good," said Wisdom Keeper. "The otter is a reminder not to worry about life, but to let it unfold, enjoying your experiences without fear."

 Power Stick

Then Wisdom Keeper bent down and handed Looks Within a long stick.

"We will create your power stick from this staff," Wisdom Keeper said. "We will decorate it with ribbons of white, green, yellow, and black, the colors of the four directions. And we will tie a bell to the stick, so when you hit the stick on the ground you wake up Mother Nature to say, 'I'm here, I am a daughter of the earth!'"

Q ❧ Quill

Wisdom Keeper motioned with her chin in the direction of the porcupine rubbing against a dried log, scratching its back.

"Looks Within," Wisdom Keeper began, "the quills from the porcupine were beautifully and skillfully woven onto your bag. The porcupine uses its quills for protection. Humans use words sometimes as quills, throwing them out quickly, never to be retrieved. Be careful with your words, for they can pierce deeply and cause much pain. With skill, words can be used to open others' hearts."

R Rock

Sitting by the side of the pond, Wisdom Keeper stooped over to pick up a rock. "Everything has life, including this rock," she said, holding it out to Looks Within. "Everything has a spirit. A rock can stand on each of its sides with a little coaxing; try it." And Looks Within practiced balancing her rock on each of its five sides.

S Seashell

As they looked at the pond, Wisdom Keeper pulled a seashell from her bag and put it in Looks Within's hand. "Most of the earth is covered with water. The seashell will bring you rhythm, like the waves that slowly moved in and out of it. Place this in your quilled bag, Looks Within."

T Turtle

A turtle moved into the water. "What about the turtle?" asked Looks Within. "Does it bring a reminder?"

"Turtle has a hard shell for protection, and moves slowly. Your brother's spirit bag, which contains his umbilical cord, is in the shape of a turtle for a long, protected life."

U Utensil

As they began to walk again, they passed a stick; Wisdom Keeper picked it up. A little later they passed a rock, and she picked that up also. "What utensils can we make from these?" she asked.

"The stick could be a planting tool, and the rock…" Looks Within considered. "The rock might be used for breaking hulls."

"Very good," said Wisdom Keeper. "But when we combine them, they have a different use: They make a utensil for mashing chokecherries.

"When we see the stick as a stick, Looks Within, and the rock as a rock, we make a judgment—much as we do with people when we do not know why they have met us on our path of life. But there is always a reason."

V | Vision Quest

"You are not old enough yet, Looks Within, but one day you will go on a vision quest to look for your purpose and direction in life," Wisdom Keeper said as they walked along. "I will take you out to the grassy meadow, where you will spend four days and nights without food or sleep, until you see your reason for being here on this earth. But for now, it is not time."

W Water

Wisdom Keeper pointed to the water of the pond. "Looks Within, take a rock, pretend it's your anger, and throw it into the calm water." Looks Within did as she was told. Fish jumped, dragonflies flew, and waves crashed on the rocks. Wisdom Keeper nodded. "Now, with the same anger, throw a pebble," she said. Looks Within threw a pebble into the water. Tiny rings formed, gently rippling toward the bank.

"What we put out affects all that is around us. Think about it: Do you want to be a ripple or a wave?" asked Wisdom Keeper.

X Symbol for Crossroad

They walked on, until they came to the crossroad. Taking her stick, Wisdom Keeper drew an X on the ground.

"When you come to a crossroad, you must choose which way to go," she said. "Your life will be filled with such choices. You will make some good ones and some bad, but all of us must choose for ourselves, and we are all responsible for our own choices. Watch the way your decisions turn out, and learn from them."

Y Yarrow

As they headed back to the place where their walk began, Wisdom Keeper pointed to a plant growing nearby. "Yarrow is a medicine that helps to heal wounds. The plant kingdom offers many, many medicines to use along the path."

She stood quietly for a moment with her walking stick in hand. "Did you like the secrets you learned on the path, Looks Within?" she asked.

Looks Within nodded.

Z Zest

"If you honor the gifts from this day, and carry them in your heart, you will have a new zest for living," said Wisdom Keeper. From her bag she took an abalone shell and some dried cedar. She placed the cedar on the shell and lit it. The cedar smoldered, sending a stream of fragrant smoke into the air.

Looks Within took her eagle feather from her carrying case. She held it above her head and whispered her message: "Great Spirit, Great Spirit, look down upon the earth and recognize my face. Great Spirit, Great Spirit, I know that we are one."